This Little Tiger book belongs to:

_____

_____

_____

For Louise and Eloise,
my inspiration and energy - J L

LITTLE TIGER PRESS LTD,
an imprint of the Little Tiger Group
1 Coda Studios, 189 Munster Road,
London SW6 6AW
www.littletiger.co.uk

First published in Great Britain 2016
This edition published 2016

A CIP catalogue record for this book is available
from the British Library

Printed in China • LTP/2700/2574/1118

3 5 7 9 10 8 6 4

Jonny Lambert

Little
Why

LITTLE TIGER

LONDON

At the back and in-between the Elders,
Little Why walked in line . . .

. . . well almost!

"Keep in line!"

Back in line,
Little Why spied Wildebeest.

"Wow!" Little Why gasped.

"I need some spiny-spiky special horns like those!"

"I would look super-duper scary!"

"I would charge this way and that!"

"Could I have some spiny-spiky special horns?"

"NO!"

"Why?"

"Keep in line!"

Back in line,
Little Why
spotted Giraffe.

"Cor!" Little Why
gasped.

"I've got to get some long-lofty leggy legs like those!"

"I would be
super-stretchy tall!"
squeaked Little Why.

"I could reach the highest leaves!"

"I could see for miles!"

"Could I have some long-lofty leggy legs?"

"NO!"

"Why?"

"Keep in line!"

Back in line . . .

. . . Little Why spied Cheetah.

"Crikey, I want speedy-spotty, fuzzy fur like that!"

"Could I have some speedy-spotty, fuzzy fur?"

"NO!"

"Why?"

"Keep in line!"

NOT back in line, Little Why spotted Crocodile.

"Wow! What a snippy-snappy snazzy snout!
Could I have a . . ."

"Little Why,
you HAVE
to stay
in line!"

Back in line,
Little Why
sulked.

"If only I had fancy feathers,
I could flutter and
fly away like Bird.
If only . . ."

"... we're here!

You don't need spotty fur or spiky horns, Little Why. You've got fantastic flippy-flappy ears, a super-squirty trunk and ..."

"... you're **special** just the way you are!"